PEGGY LITTLE-LEGS

PIP JONES

Illustrated by
Paula Bowles

Barrington Stoke

First published in 2023 in Great Britain by
Barrington Stoke Ltd
18 Walker Street, Edinburgh, EH3 7LP

www.barringtonstoke.co.uk

Text © 2023 Pip Jones
Illustrations © 2023 Paula Bowles

A CIP catalogue record for this book is available
from the British Library upon request

ISBN: 978-1-80090-214-5

Printed by Hussar Books, Poland

This book is in a super-readable format for young readers
beginning their independent reading journey.

For my nieces, Martha and Evie xx

CONTENTS

CHAPTER 1
The adventure begins

Peggy didn't know if she was nervous or excited.

"It's happening at last!" she yapped to her friend, Bobbin. "Puppy School Adventure Weekend, here we come!"

"Quiet please, everypup!" Mrs Floof barked. "Listen while I tell you what this weekend is all about."

The puppies sat around Mrs Floof to listen. Peggy tried to stop her tail wagging, but she couldn't. It tapped loudly all the time Mrs Floof was talking.

"You're here," Mrs Floof went on, "to practise some important puppy skills before you go and live with your new owners – and the best pup this weekend will win a prize!"

"The prize is a MegaBone Biscuit!" Bobbin whispered to the others, licking his lips.

"A MegaBone Biscuit?" yapped Wade – a large, shaggy brown puppy next to Bobbin. "I've never seen one of those, but my big brother told me they're the biggest, yummiest treats ever!"

"ARFF! ARFF!" Mrs Floof woofed loudly so that the puppies would stop yapping and calm down.

"Today, we'll be doing fast running and jumping through hoops and over fences. Tonight, we'll camp in the woods, then tomorrow, we'll do a long walk along the top of Grim Gully."

The puppies wriggled nervously.

"My mum said it's ever so steep," Bobbin blurted.

"Let's not worry about the gully until tomorrow," Peggy said. "Today is going to be so much fun! Yip-yip-yippee!"

CHAPTER 2
Ready, steady ...

The field the puppies were now in was so enormous, Peggy could hardly see the wooden fence at the other end.

Next to Peggy, Bobbin was zooming in circles, chasing his tail.

"Bobbin, stop that!" Mrs Floof ordered. "You'll never catch it!"

"I'm sure I will *one* day," Bobbin panted.

"Let's use up some of your energy," Mrs Floof said, "with a running race!"

"Oh, hooray!" came a silky voice next to Peggy. "Running is my favourite!"

Peggy stared up at the tall, beautiful pup next to her. She had silver-grey fur and long, strong back legs.

"I'm Wisp!" the dog said, and sniffed Peggy's nose to say hello. "I'm a whippet, and running is what whippets do best!"

"That's so cool," Peggy replied. "I'm a sausage dog, and I don't know what we do best."

"This is where the race will start AND finish," Mrs Floof said. She used a big paw to flatten the grass, and one by one the puppies lined up where she showed them.

"Run past that big tree, all the way to the fence at the end and then back again – as fast as you can!" Mrs Floof barked.

Wisp bent her head down to the ground and waited for the race to begin. Nora's back paws scratched at the grass. Peggy's tail wagged fast and loud. She'd never run in a proper race before.

Mrs Floof looked across at the puppies ...

"Ready, pups? Three, two, one ..."

CHAPTER 3
GO!

"GO!"

All the puppies sped off. Peggy's ears flapped in the breeze, and her tiny paws pounded on the turf.

"Wah!" Peggy gasped as Wisp zoomed past her.

In a second, the whippet was almost out of sight.

"Run, run, run!" Peggy panted. She longed for her little legs to go quicker, but all the other pups were faster.

One by one, they overtook her. She'd only just passed the big tree when Wisp whizzed past her again – this time on her way back to the finish line.

Peggy grunted and pushed on until
her nose touched the fence at the end.
She stood there for a moment, panting.

"It's such a long way!" she gasped out loud – but no one was there to hear her. The other puppies had almost finished the race.

"Running," Peggy puffed, "is definitely *not* my favourite!"

By the time Peggy got back to the finish line, Bobbin was chasing his tail again.

The other pups were rolling on their tummies and chasing butterflies, waiting for Peggy.

"Last but not least," Mrs Floof called, "here's Peggy!"

"Gosh, you really *are* the best at running, Wisp!" Peggy puffed. "I've never seen a pup run as fast as that!"

"Told you!" Wisp replied proudly. "But you did really well too – for a pup with legs as little as yours."

CHAPTER 4
Bouncy-bouncing

Peggy looked down at her little legs and huffed.

"These weren't much good at running fast," she groaned, and wiggled one front leg at Bobbin.

"Don't worry!" Bobbin replied. "The next challenge isn't about being fast; it's about bouncy-bouncing. And bouncy-bouncing is

    so

        much

                fun!"

Bobbin boinged round and round Peggy in a circle.

Peggy looked at all the equipment Mrs Floof had set up.

There were three white fences, all different sizes, and a line of orange and white cones which led to four hoops that hung from the branches of a tree.

"It does look sort of fun," Peggy murmured, "but some of those hoops and fences are ever so high. How will I ever get over *that* one?"

Peggy nodded at the largest fence, which was as high as Wade's head.

"Remember, this challenge is about agility, not speed," Mrs Floof explained to the puppies, who yipped excitedly – all except Peggy. "You need to be nifty – and that means be aware of your paws and tails at all times."

"Can I go first, pleeeease?" Bobbin asked.

Peggy watched as her friend bounded around the course. He was amazing! He sprang over the fences, zigzagged through the cones, then hurtled through the hoops. Everyone cheered when he did a bouncy twirl at the end.

"It's like you have springs in your paws!" Wade giggled.

Watching Bobbin had made Peggy feel so nervous, her ears drooped, and while everyone was busy watching Nora, Peggy went and sat behind Wade.

Maybe if I hide here, Mrs Floof will forget I haven't had my turn, she thought. But then ...

"Peggy Little-Legs! Come to the front. It's your go."

CHAPTER 5
Boing, boing, crash!

Peggy's knees wobbled as she stepped out from behind Wade and walked to the front.

"Don't worry, Peggy!" Bobbin called. "Just do your best!"

"You can do this," Peggy told herself. She took a very deep breath, then ran towards the first fence and ... JUMPED!

"Yes! I did it!" she yipped as she bounced over and landed on the grass.

The next one was a bit bigger. Peggy leapt as high as she could, but her back foot caught the top of the fence as she was landing and knocked it over.

Peggy already knew she wasn't going to make it over the third and highest fence, but she was running too fast to stop.

"OUCH!" she yipped as her long snout bashed into the wood. The fence toppled over with Peggy on top.

"Don't worry, Peggy," Mrs Floof called. "Just keep going – the cones next!"

"Silly little legs," Peggy growled to herself. She gave her ears a good shake and then trotted to the cones.

"Remember, you have to zigzag!" Bobbin shouted, trying to help.

Bobbin had made the zigzagging look easy. But it wasn't. While the front of Peggy's long body was zigging past the third cone, the back of her body was still zagging past the second one.

"Grrr! I've knocked nearly all of them over!"

"It doesn't matter," Mrs Floof called. "Try the hoops."

The hoops were swaying to and fro in the breeze, and sometimes they banged into each other. Peggy's tail wagged just a little.

If I time it right, Peggy thought, *I might be able to get through them two at a time!*

She watched and waited – and when she saw the two hoops swinging towards each other, she ran for it.

"Wooo!" Bobbin cheered.

For a moment, Peggy thought she actually might make it through, but then ...

"Oh, noooo!"

The hoops swung in opposite directions, separating just as she was trying to jump through them. Her front legs hooked over one hoop, and her back legs over the other.

Peggy was stuck! Dangling from a tree between two hoops, swaying in the breeze and feeling very silly indeed.

"Help," she said quietly.

Peggy felt her tail droop as she waited for Mrs Floof to come and get her down.

CHAPTER 6
Back at camp

All the pups had scoffed a bowl of crunchy kibble for dinner. They took turns to drink from a big bowl of fresh water, then Mrs Floof asked them to choose a bed to snuggle down on.

"What a great day!" Bobbin murmured, stretching.

"You were so good on those hoops!" said Wisp, patting Bobbin's paw with her own.

"And *you* were *amazing* in the running race, Wisp!" Wade added. "Hey, who do you think will win the MegaBone Biscuit tomorrow?"

"It definitely won't be me," Peggy huffed. "I wasn't best at *anything*."

"Don't say that." Bobbin nuzzled Peggy's ear. "You did great!"

Peggy knew her friend was trying to make her feel better, but she sighed.

"I wasn't best at anything either, Peggy!" Nora piped up. "And we've still got the Grim Gully walk. Mrs Floof said the challenge tomorrow is about listening to commands."

"It's a long walk for my silly little legs," Peggy replied.

"Don't worry," Wisp said kindly. "We know today has been tricky for you, but remember we're just puppies! We've all got *lots* more growing to do. Perhaps your legs won't always be this stubby?"

"Bedtime, everypup!" Mrs Floof called.

"I'm not tired at all!" Bobbin insisted. Then he yawned, closed his eyes and quickly began snoring.

While all the other puppies drifted off to sleep, Peggy gazed up at the stars twinkling through the branches.

"I really hope the Gully walk will be easier than running and jumping," she whispered to herself. "I must be good at *something*."

CHAPTER 7
Grim Gully

A cockerel crowing from a farm woke Peggy up suddenly. The other puppies were still asleep on their cosy beds.

Peggy gazed at Wisp's long, strong legs, which were so good for running.

Then she noticed Bobbin's paws were twitching as he slept, and she wondered if he was dreaming about bouncy-bouncing, which he loved so much – and he was so good at.

"Wake up, everypup!" Mrs Floof yelled.

The puppies' eyes blinked and opened. They all yawned and stretched.

"Good morning, Bobbin," Peggy said, nuzzling his ear. "Sorry I was grumpy last night."

Bobbin scratched his tummy and then licked Peggy's face all over with his big, sloppy tongue.

"Hey!" she yipped. "Not my eyeballs!"

"We'll have a happy day today," Bobbin said. "I'll walk next to you all the way."

After breakfast, Mrs Floof told the puppies to sit around her.

"The walk to the top of Grim Gully is steep and stony," she said, making sure the pups were all listening. "And at the top, we have to stay well away from the edge. Today is about being slow and steady, listening to what I tell you, and looking after each other, OK? Let's go."

Mrs Floof led the puppies to the bottom of a steep path.

"Wow, Bobbin!" Peggy whispered. "Look how far up we have to go!"

The thick tree branches overhead meant the path was cool and shady but, even so, it wasn't long before Peggy was

out of breath and her little legs were very tired. Bobbin panted next to her.

Slowly the dogs made their way up, up, up, careful not to trip on the rocks and tree roots that stuck out of the ground.

"We're nearly at the top!" Mrs Floof called at last.

As soon as the path flattened out, Wisp dashed ahead.

"How exciting!" she yapped. "We're really high!"

"NO RUNNING!" Mrs Floof barked. "It's not safe!"

But Wisp was already running – because running was what Wisp did best.

CHAPTER 8
The drop

"STOP!"

Mrs Floof growled at Wisp, but the whippet had bounded a long way ahead.

Peggy gasped when she saw Wisp's back paws skid on the gravel.

Wisp yelped as her rear end slid sideways. She clawed at the ground with her front paws, trying to stop herself from falling, but it was too late. In an instant she'd dropped out of sight and vanished.

"Wiiiiisp!" Peggy squealed.

Mrs Floof was running now. The puppies trotted safely behind until they caught up.

Peggy peered down. Far below, she could just about see Wisp, who had fallen into a deep crack in the rock face. It looked very dim, damp and scary.

"Wisp, can you hear me?" Mrs Floof called out. "Are you all right?"

"My paws hurt," Wisp whined. "And I bumped my head. How am I going to get out of this hole?"

"I'm going to drop a rope down to you," Mrs Floof replied. "You'll need to tie it safely around yourself, and then we'll pull you up."

With her mouth, Mrs Floof opened the kit bag that was hanging from her neck. She took out a long brown rope and quickly tied one end to a strong tree. Then she tossed the other end over the side down to Wisp.

Wisp pulled the rope towards her. She lay it over her tummy and rolled over so it went round her body – but when she tried to tie it up, she yelped.

"I can't make a knot!" she whimpered. "My paws hurt too much. What am I going to do?"

"Well, um …" Mrs Floof frowned.

"Look over there!" Peggy blurted. "Can you see? There's a little beam of light shining on Wisp's tail? I think there might be another way into that hole."

"You're right!" Mrs Floof gasped. "Puppies, follow me. We need to find a safe way down to the bottom of the gully – everyone stick together."

CHAPTER 9
Hero

Very slowly, following Mrs Floof and walking nose to tail, the puppies made their way along a steep and craggy trail, down, down, down to the bottom of the gully.

"Bark if you can hear me, Wisp!" Mrs Floof shouted. "We're trying to find a way in to reach you!"

"Arff! Arff!" came a far-away woof.

"There!" Peggy said. "That's the way in. Bobbin, pull back those weeds."

Bobbin squashed the weeds with his paw. Behind them was a gap in the rock. Peggy pushed her long snout inside and sniffed.

"She's definitely in there," Peggy insisted. "I can smell her!"

"But how will we get to her?" Nora asked. "That gap is tiny! There's no way Mrs Floof can fit through it."

Peggy looked down at her little legs, and then at the crack.

"The opening *is* tiny," she said. "But so am I. I think I could fit through there. Can I try, Mrs Floof? Wisp must be so scared."

"No, Peggy!" Bobbin sniffled. "What if you get stuck as well? Mrs Floof said we all have to stay together."

"I really think I can do it," Peggy told Miss Floof. "Wisp won't be able to fit through that gap either, but if I can just get to her, I can tie the rope, and then you can pull us up."

"Well," Mrs Floof said after a moment, "you're a very brave puppy, Peggy, and I think you can do it too. I'll take the other pups back to the top. Good luck."

CHAPTER 10
Into the dark

Peggy watched Mrs Floof begin to lead the pups back up the steep trail, then she took a deep breath and pushed her head inside the gap in the rock.

She crouched and crawled inside, blinking in the darkness.

"I'm going to have to follow my nose," Peggy whispered to herself as she inched forwards, deeper and deeper into the cliff, sniffing as she went.

The cool ground scraped Peggy's tummy, but when she reached a bend, the tunnel opened up a little.

"Wisp!" Peggy called. "Can you hear me? I'm coming!"

"I'm here!" Wisp called back. "This way!"

Shivering now, Peggy followed the sound of Wisp's call.

"Is Peggy there yet, Wisp?"

Peggy heard Mrs Floof's booming voice echo through the underground tunnels, and she knew she was going the right way.

Suddenly, she saw light ahead. She sped forwards and when she turned one more corner ...

"Found you!"

"Peggy!" Wisp cried. "You're the best!"

High above, Mrs Floof and the other pups cheered.

"You did it!" Bobbin exclaimed. "I knew you would!"

Peggy tied the rope around Wisp, and then around her own tummy as well. She tugged to make sure it was nice and tight.

"Ready!" she called.

Wisp nuzzled Peggy's ear as Mrs Floof tugged hard on the rope, lifting them off the ground and slowly all the way to the top, where Bobbin was bouncing on the spot.

"I think that's enough walking for today," Mrs Floof sighed happily. "Let's go back to camp and have a rest before we go home."

Back at camp, Mrs Floof handed out little treats which the puppies scoffed up.

"It's been an exciting weekend!" she said. "You've all done brilliantly and learned about your own special skills – but I only have one MegaBone Biscuit prize."

All the pups' tails wagged.

"I bet I know who's won it!" Bobbin blurted.

"Me too!"

"Me too!"

"And me!"

"Some pups are best at running or bouncy-bouncing," Bobbin said, "but Peggy's best at being a hero!"

"Quite right!" Mrs Floof replied, and Peggy gasped when Mrs Floof gave her the huge, delicious prize.

"I can't eat all this!" she giggled. "I'm *far* too little! I think that everypup should share it."

And they did.